Wide Awake

Julie Paschkis

Henry Holt and Company
New York

To Julian

All of the animals
are wide awake.

The snake slithers.

The pig prances.

The butterfly flutters by.

The raven is restless.

The dog is dizzy.

Even the whale

is wide awake.

Wake up, now

Now, sleep well.

is still.

Even the songbird

The bee barely buzzes.

The salamander slumbers.

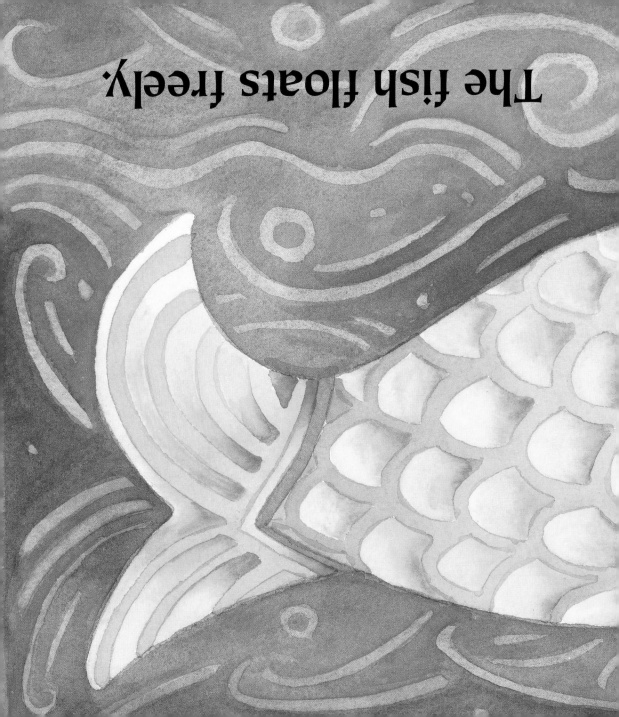

The fish floats freely.

The rabbit rests.

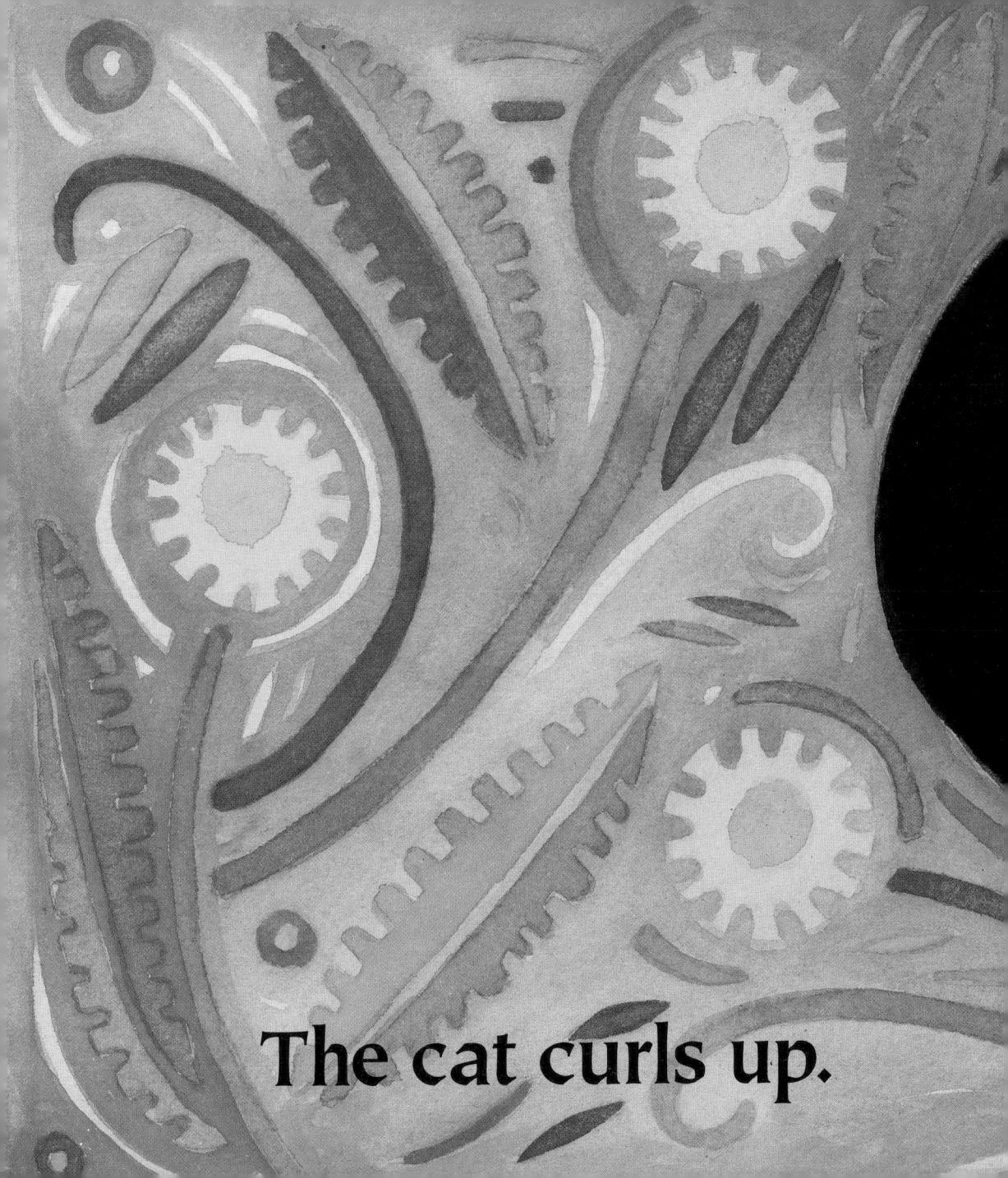

The cat curls up.

All of the animals are
so sleepy.

To Joe Max

Henry Holt and Company, Inc., *Publishers since 1866*, 115 West 18th Street,
New York, New York 10011. Henry Holt is a registered trademark of Henry Holt
and Company, Inc. Copyright © 1994 by Julie Paschkis. All rights reserved. Published in
Canada by Fitzhenry & Whiteside Ltd., 195 Allstate Parkway, Markham, Ontario L3R 4T8.
Library of Congress Cataloging-in-Publication Data: Paschkis, Julie. [So sleepy] / So sleepy;
Wide awake/Julie Paschkis. Summary: In the first half of this book, animals sleep; in the
second half, they wake up. The two stories are printed in opposite directions.
1. Upside-down books—Specimens. [1. Sleep—Fiction. 2. Animals—Fiction. 3. Upside-down
books. 4. Toy and movable books.] I. Title. II. Title: So sleepy. III. Title: Wide awake.
PZ7.P2686So 1994 [E]—dc20 93-47046 ISBN 0-8050-3174-X First Edition—1994
Printed in the United States of America on acid-free paper. ∞
1 3 5 7 9 10 8 6 4 2
The paintings for this book were created with
Windsor & Newton gouache on Arches watercolor paper.

So Sleepy

Julie Paschkis

Henry Holt and Company
New York